The following eBook is reproduced below with the goal of providing information that is as accurate and as reliable as possible. Regardless, purchasing this eBook can be seen as consent to the fact that both the publisher and the author of this book are in no way experts on the topics discussed within, and that any recommendations or suggestions made herein are for entertainment purposes only. Professionals should be consulted as needed before undertaking any of the action endorsed herein.

This declaration is deemed fair and valid by both the American Bar Association and the Committee of Publishers Association and is legally binding throughout the United States.

Furthermore, the transmission, duplication or reproduction of any of the following work, including precise information, will be considered an illegal act, irrespective whether it is done electronically or in print. The legality extends to creating a secondary or tertiary copy of the work or a recorded copy and is only allowed with express written consent of the Publisher. All additional rights are reserved.

The information in the following pages is broadly considered to be a truthful and accurate account of facts, and as such any inattention, use or misuse of the information in question by the reader will render any resulting actions solely under their purview. There are no scenarios in which the publisher or the original author of this work can be in any fashion deemed liable for any hardship or damages that may befall them after undertaking information described herein.

Additionally, the information found on the following pages is intended for informational purposes only and should thus be considered, universal. As befitting its nature, the information presented is without assurance regarding its continued validity or interim quality. Trademarks that mentioned are done without written consent and can in no way be considered an endorsement from the trademark holder.

# Introduction

Congratulations on downloading your personal copy of *Serial Killers*. Thank you for doing so.

The following chapters will discuss many events of the infamous serial killer Jeffrey Dahmer's life.

You will discover the life that led up to Jeffrey's murders, the murders he committed, and then the trial and aftermath of his story.

The final chapter will talk about how things ended up for Dahmer and how it has affected other people.

There are plenty of books on this subject on the market, thanks again for choosing this one! Every effort was made to ensure it is full of as much useful information as possible. Please enjoy!

Congratulations on downloading your personal copy of *Serial Killers*. Thank you for doing so.

# Part 1: His Beginnings

## Early Life

At the Evangelical Deaconess Hospital in West Allis, Wisconsin, on May 21, 1960, at 4:34 PM, Jeffrey Dahmer was born. His parents were Lionel Herbert Dahmer and Joyce Annette. At the time of his birth, his father was going for a chemistry degree at Marquette University. His mother was teletype machine instructor.

Even though both parents doted upon Dahmer when he was young, Joyce was often argumentative, tense, and in constant need of attention when it came to her neighbors and husband. Since Lionel was away a lot, raising Jeffrey put a lot of stress on Joyce, so Lionel moved his family in with his mother so that she could help out.

When Jeffrey started first grade, Joyce spent a growing amount of time in her bed because of weakness. Lionel was away a lot because of his studies, and when he was home, Joyce demanded his full attention. It was reported that she often works up her anxiety over simple problems just to get her husband to give her his undivided attention. Joyce Dahmer, at one point, tried to commit suicide by overdosing on Equanil, to which she was addicted to. Because of these problems, neither one of them spent much time with Jeffrey.

Dahmer had always been considered a happy and energetic child, but he became more subdued after he had to undergo a double hernia surgery just before his fourth birthday. Nobody took the time to explain to him what was going on. The operation left him feeling scared because of the strangers that kept coming up to him and checking his body. In his later life, Dahmer recalled that his early years had been extremely tensed, which he said was from his parents. This was because he constantly noticed them arguing.

In elementary school, his peers looked at him as timid and quiet. In a report card during the first-grade, a teacher referred to him as a child who was reserved and who she thought felt neglected. The teacher further noted that the neglect seemed to be caused by his mother's health problems. Even though he was mainly uncommunicative and reserved, he did have a few friends.

Early on in his life, Dahmer became interested in animals. His friends would later recall that Dahmer started out collecting large insects, butterflies, and dragonflies, which he kept in jars. Then, later on, sometimes with friends, Dahmer would start collecting animal carcasses that he found on the side of the road. Dahmer would dismember these animals either at his house or in a small wooded area behind his home. One of his friends said that he would take the animals apart and keep them stored in jars and keep them in the tool shed. He would always explain that he was only curious as to how the parts of the animals fit together. On one occasion, he impaled a head of a dog on a stake that was behind the house.

This fascination with animals likely started when, around four, he remembered his father getting rid of animal bones that were under the family's home. Lionel said that he found his son fascinated by the sounds the bones, which made him became fixated with collecting and playing with animal bones. He began searching around the house to find more bones. He would also explore living animals, and try and locate where their bones were.

In October 1966 the Dahmers moved to Doylestown, Ohio. During this move, Joyce was pregnant with their second son. On December 18, 1966, she gave birth to another boy, and they allowed Jeffrey to pick his little brother's name. He picked the name, David. Even though he picked his brother's name, Dahmer kept neutral feelings towards his brother and they never really became close. Lionel also received his degree that year and became employed in Akron as an analytical chemist.

The family moved to Bath, Ohio in 1968. Shortly after they moved in, Dahmer was molested by a boy neighbor. This went unreported at the time and may have played a big part in Dahmer's subsequent actions. Two years after that, the family was having chicken for dinner, and Dahmer inquired to his dad what a bleach bath would do to the bones. By this point, Lionel had become worried about his oldest son's lazy and placid mood, and his solitary existence. Therefore, he was happy that he son was showing initiative to, what he thought, was a scientific curiosity. He happily showed his son the way to carefully and safely use bleach, and then later on, how to preserve animal bones. Dahmer would then use this knowledge about cleaning and preserving bones on a lot of the animal remains that he had been collecting.

## Adolescence

From the beginning of his time at Revere High School, Dahmer had little friends and was seen as an outcast. Several of his former classmates shared later that they found it disturbing that he drank beer and spirits. He would smuggle then into school hidden in the lining of the army fatigue jacket he always wore, and then he would secretly conceal in his school locker. The abuse of alcohol would often happen before, during, and after school, and was noted first when he was 14. His drinking may have started as a way for him to make friends. A classmate observed, on one occasion, Dahmer drinking a glass of gin and questioned as to why he drank in class. Dahmer responded by saying, "It's my medicine." Despite this, during his freshman year, Dahmer, mainly uncommunicative, was seen by the staff as a polite student who was also very intelligent. He started out only having average grades, and the staff believed this was caused by his apathy. He also participated in tennis, and he may have, for a short while, been a part of the high school band.

Many of his peers tried to keep their distance because they found him strange. He talked differently, and he had a short temper. He discovered that when he acted differently, such as making a public scene, people watched him and he would have their attention. Jeffrey also liked to trace bodies on the floor of the classroom. After this, his classmates realized that he was more than just a little weird.

Once Dahmer reached puberty, he realized that he was homosexual. He didn't tell his parents about his sexual orientation. He had a relationship with a fellow student during his early teens, but they never engaged in intercourse. He later admitted that as he started to have sexual fantasies, problems of control and dominance over a subservient partner were a big part of his thoughts. This then slowly became intertwined with his fascination of dissection.

When he was around 16, he thought up a fantasy about raping a male jogger that he thought was attractive by knocking him out and then sexually abusing the unconscious body. He decided to try to achieve this fantasy, so to render him unconscious, Dahmer waited in the bushes along the route that he knew the jogger took. He had a baseball bat readied and waited for the jogger to come along. On the day he had chosen to wait, the jogger didn't pass by. Even though he never tried to attempt this again, Dahmer later admitted that this was his first attack attempt on an individual.

Even though most of his peers viewed him as an oddball and a loner, Dahmer still became known as a class clown of sorts because of the pranks he liked to stage regularly. Most of these pranks were only to make others laugh, while others were just to get attention. His peers would start to call these pranks as "Doing a Dahmer" and included things like knocking things over at stores and school, simulating cerebral palsy or epileptic seizures, or bleating. Dahmer's grades had started to decline by 1977, mainly because of his growing abuse of alcohol and his disregard toward social and academic interactions.

Dahmer's parents hired him a tutor, but they only had limited success. During this same time, his parents began going to counseling to try and work through some problems and reconcile their marriage. This ended up being unsuccessful, and they ended up getting divorced. The divorce began amicably, but soon both parents started to quarrel more frequently in front of their children. Lionel moved out in early 1978.

In May of 1978, Dahmer graduated high school. A couple of weeks before the graduation, a teacher noticed Dahmer sitting near the parking lot of the school drinking many beers. This teacher threatened to turn him in, and Dahmer told the teacher that he had been experiencing family problems and the counselor knew what was going on. Not long after this, Joyce was awarded custody of the younger boy and moved away to live with some family. Since Jeffrey was now 18, and a legal adult, and not part of the consideration of the court.

## Early Adulthood

During the summer of 1978, at 18 years old, Dahmer committed his first murder three weeks after he graduated from high school. During this time, he was living by himself at the family home. Dahmer's father had been temporarily living in a nearby motel, and Joyce went to Chippewa Falls, Wisconsin along with David. Dahmer picked up a hitchhiker, 18-year-old Steven Mark Hicks, on June 18.

He was able to lure the youth to his house by telling him they would drink alcohol. Hicks had been on his way to a concert in Lockwood Corners when he said he would go back to Dahmer's place. Dahmer later said that after they had been listening to music and drinking for several hours, "Hicks wanted to leave and I didn't want him to." This led to Jeffrey bludgeoning him to death using a 10-pound dumbbell. Later, Dahmer would state that he hit Hicks two times from the back while Hicks was sitting in a chair. After he was unconscious, Dahmer strangled him with the same dumbbell bar. After he was dead, Dahmer removed Hicks' clothing before masturbating while standing over the corpse.

The next day, Dahmer would dissect the body in the house's crawl space and place the remains in a shallow grave in the backyard. Several weeks later, he dug up the remains and took the flesh off the bones. He then placed the skin in some acid for it to dissolve and then flushed it. He used a sledgehammer to crush up the bones and then scattered them in the woods.

Lionel and his fiancée came back to the family home six weeks after Hicks' murder where they found Dahmer living alone. Dahmer enrolled at Ohio State University that August and hoped to major in business. The whole time Dahmer was enrolled, he was unproductive due to his alcohol abuse. Lionel said, on one occasion, he visited his son and found his room covered in empty liquor bottles. Even though his father had already paid for another term, Dahmer dropped out after only attending for three months.

After urging from his father, Dahmer enlisted in the US Army in January 1979 and trained at Fort Sam Houston as a medical specialist. He was then stationed in Baumholder, West Germany on July 13, 1979, and served as a combat medic. Dahmer was considered an "average or slightly above average" soldier during his first year of service. Two soldiers did claim that Dahmer raped them. In 2010, one stated that while in Baumholder; he had repeatedly been raped by Dahmer during a span of 17-months, while the other said he thought he had been drugged, then Dahmer raped him in 1979 inside an armored personnel carrier. Dahmer's performance began to deteriorate due to his alcohol abuse. This led to him being deemed unfit for military service in March 1981 and later received an honorable discharge because he superiors didn't think that the problems he had exhibited would be applicable in a civilian life.

He was subsequently sent to Fort Jackson on March 24, 1981, for debriefing and then they gave him a ticket to travel to any US city. He would later tell police that he couldn't return home because he didn't want to face his father, so instead, he went to Miami Beach. He explained that he was "tired of the cold" and wanted to see if he could live on his own. Dahmer was able to find employment in Florida at a delicatessen and rented a motel room. He spent most of his money on alcohol, he was quickly kicked out because of nonpayment. He first began spending his evenings at the beach while still working, but he called his father in September of 1981 and asked to go back to Ohio.

Once he was back in Ohio, Dahmer first lived with his stepmother and father and insisted that they give him a lot of chores to take up his time as he was searching for a job, but he still continued to drink. Two weeks after he had returned to Ohio, Dahmer ended up getting arrested and charged with being drunk and disorderly. He received a suspended ten-day sentence and $60 fine. His father tried to get him off of alcohol but without success. He was sent to live with his grandmother in West Allis in December of 1981. His grandmother was the only person that he ever showed affection towards. They had hoped that her influence, and a change of location, would help Dahmer to give up alcohol, live responsibly, and find a job.

Dahmer and his grandmother's living arrangements started out harmoniously. He would go to church with her, willingly did chores, looked for work, and followed her house rules, but he still drank. Her influence did bring about results, and he found a phlebotomist job in 1982 at a blood plasma center in Milwaukee. He was able to keep the job for ten months before he was laid off. After this, he was unemployed for more than two years, and during this time he lived off the money that he was given by his grandmother.

Dahmer was arrested for indecent exposure just before he lost his job. While at the Wisconsin State Fair Park, on August 7, 1982, he was seen exposing himself in front of 25 children and women. He received a $50 fine for this conviction.

He finally found a job in January 1985 when he was hired at the Milwaukee Ambrosia Chocolate Factory as a mixer. Here, he worked from 11PM to 7AM, with only Saturdays off. A short time after he got the job, an incident happened at the West Allis Public Library where he was proposition by a man while reading. The man tossed him a note that offered to perform fellatio. Even though he didn't respond, this caused his fantasies of dominance for his adolescence to stir, and he started to become familiar with the local gay baths, bathhouses, and bookstores. He even stole a male mannequin that he used for sexual stimulation for a short time before his grandmother found it in his closet and made him get rid of it.

He started to frequent the local bathhouses by late 1985, and would later describe them as relaxing, but he became frustrated by the fact that his partners would move during their sexual acts. He made a comment after his arrest that "I trained myself to view people as objects of pleasure instead of (as) people." Because of this, he began giving his partner's sleeping pills starting in June 1986. He would then rape the unconscious bodies. After around 12 incidents, the bathhouse ended up revoking his membership, so he began to rent hotel rooms. After he had been kicked out of the bathhouses, he read a newspaper article about the funeral an 18-year-old man. He began envisioning the idea of stealing the body and bring back home. Jeffrey said he did attempt to dig the coffin up, but the soil was too hard, and he gave up.

Dahmer was arrested again in August 1986 for at the Kinnickinnic River in front of two 12-year-olds. He first admitted to the offense and was charged with indecent exposure, but then he switched his story saying that he was urinating and didn't realize that there was somebody around. They then switched his offense to disorderly conduct, and he was then sentenced to a year of probation on March 10, 1987, and was instructed to undergo therapy.

# Part 2: The Murders

## Beginning of the Murders

Still residing with his grandmother, in November of 1987 he met Steven Tuomi, 25, at a gay bar and talked him into going back to the Ambassador Hotel. Jeffrey later said that he hadn't planned on killing Tuomi. He only wanted to drug and rape him. The next morning, Dahmer awoke and found Tuomi underneath the bed with blood coming from his mouth and his chest crushed. He also noticed there were bruises on his own forearm and fists. Dahmer didn't have any memory of what had happened and didn't remember killing him. He told investigators later that he couldn't believe that it had happened.

He bought a large suitcase and placed Tuomi's body inside so that he could transport it to his grandmother's house. After a week, he removed the head, arms, and legs from the body. He took the skin off the bones and cut it into small pieces, enough pieces, that he could handle. He stored the flesh in garbage bags. He placed the bones in a sheet and then broke them up with a sledgehammer. This whole process took him around two hours to finish, and everything, except for the head, was disposed of in the trash.

Dahmer kept Tuomi's head wrapped in a blanket for two weeks after his murder. He then boiled the head in Soilex and bleach mixture trying to preserve the skull, which he used for masturbation. After a while, the skull became too brittle because of the cleaning, and he eventually broke it up and got rid of it.

After his experience with Tuomi, Jeffrey started to actively look for victims, mainly at local gay bars. Most of which he talked into coming to his grandmother's place, and then he drugged them and engaged in sexual activities with their lifeless bodies. After he gave them sleeping pills to render them unconscious, he would strangle them.

Two months from Steven Tuomi's murder, Dahmer came across a James Doxtator, a 14-year-old Native American prostitute. He lured him to his residence by promising him $50 if would pose for pictures. At his residence, they had sex before Dahmer drugged him and then strangled him in the cellar. Dahmer kept the body there for a week before he took it apart just like he had with Tuomi's. He placed all of the body, except for the skull, in the garbage. After cleaning the skull, he kept it for a bit before breaking it up. He met Rich Guerrero, 22 and bisexual, on March 24, 1988, outside of The Phoenix, a gay bar. Dahmer lured him to his grandmother's place, the incentive this time being $50 to spend the night. Dahmer gave him sleeping pills and then used a leather strap to strangle him. He then had oral sex with the corpse. 24 hours later, Dahmer dismembered Guerrero's body, again disposing of the remains in the garbage and retaining the skull before getting rid of it about a month later.

Dahmer lured another man to his place of residence on April 23, but after the victim had drunk the drugged coffee, they both heard Dahmer's grandmother called out, "Is that you, Jeff?" Even though he responded in a way that would make her think he was alone, she still observed that he wasn't. This time Dahmer opted not to kill this person because of his grandmother's intrusion. He instead waited until he was unconscious and dropped him off at the County General Hospital.

In September of 1988, his Grandmother asked Dahmer to move out because of him bringing men home at night and the smells that were coming from her garage and basement. Dahmer moved into an apartment at North 25th Street on September 25th. The next day he was arrested for sexually fondling and drugging a 13-year-old which he had lured to his apartment by offering him money for posing nude for pictures. Dahmer was convicted of enticing a child for immoral purposes and second-degree sexual assault in January of 1989. His sentence was suspended until May 1989. He started a ten-day Easter break from work on March 20 and stayed with his grandmother during this time.

During the two months before he was sentenced and the two months after he had been convicted, Dahmer killed his fifth victim. This victim was Anthony Sears, a 24-year-old mixed-race aspiring model. Dahmer met him on March 25, 1989, at a gay bar. Later, Dahmer said that he wasn't planning on committing a crime that night, but shortly before the bar closed, Sears began to converse with him. Dahmer brought him back to his grandmother's where they then engaged in oral sex before he gave Sears sleeping pills and strangled him.

The next day, Dahmer moved the body to the bathtub where he removed the head before he tried to skin the corpse. He removed the skin and then crushed the bones up, which he got rid of him in the trash. Dahmer said that he thought Sears was "exceptionally attractive." Sears is the first victim that he permanently kept a body part of. He placed Sears' genitalia and head in acetone to preserve. He kept them stored at work in his locker. The next year, he moved back into an apartment and took the remains with him.

When Dahmer was sentenced on May 23, 1989, he was given a year in the House of Correction, along with work release so that he wouldn't lose his job, five years of probation, and he also became a registered sex offender.

He was paroled two months before his scheduled release, and thus his five years probation began. He temporarily lived with his grandmother after his release before he moved into the Oxford Apartments in May of 1990. Even though the apartment was in an area known for crime, it was furnished, located near his job, and was $300 a month with bills included, except for electricity.

## 924 North 25th Street

Dahmer left his grandmother's house again on May 14, 1990, into 924 North 25th Street, Apartment number 213. With him, he took Anthony Sears's painted genitals, skull, and scalp. After a week in his new place, he killed Raymond Smith, his sixth victim. Dahmer lured the 32-year-old into his apartment promising $50 for sex. Once in the apartment, Smith was given a drink with sleeping pills and then Dahmer strangled him with his hands. The next morning, he bought a Polaroid and used it to photograph Smith in different positions. Then he started to take the body apart in his bathroom. Dahmer placed the pelvis, legs, and arms in a container with Soilex and boiled them. This allowed him to be able to rinse everything off in the sink. He then dissolved the remaining parts of the body in a container with acid, except for the skull. He then painted the skull and set it beside Sears' skull.

Around May 27, another man was lured to Dahmer's apartment. This time, Dahmer ended up drinking the laced drink that was supposed to be for the victim. The next day when he awoke, he found that the victim had stolen some clothing, a watch, and $300. He didn't tell the police, but when he met with his probation officer on May 29, he told him that he'd been robbed.

In June 1990, Edward Smith, 27, went to Dahmer's apartment. Dahmer drugged and strangled him. This time, instead of immediately placing the skeleton in acid or following the same process as before, which had caused the skulls to become brittle, Jeffrey decided to freeze the skeleton for a few months in hopes that it would remove excess moisture. Freezing didn't get rid of the moisture, then he acidified the skeleton several months later. He accidentally destroyed the skull when he tried to dry it in the oven. This only made the skull explode. Dahmer told the police that he felt "rotten" about killing Smith because he was unable to keep any of the man's body parts.

Around three months after Smith's murder, Dahmer met Ernest Miller, a 22-year-old Chicago native, on North 27th Street. Dahmer convinced Miller to come to his apartment with the promise of $50 if he allowed him to listen to the sounds that his stomach and heart made. When Dahmer made a move towards oral sex, Miller informed him that it would cost him more. Dahmer then gave the victim a laced drink, but he only had two sleeping pills, so he killed him by slicing his throat. The knife that he used for dissecting the bodies was the same knife he used to kill Miller. Miller was dead within a few minutes from blood loss.

The body was then posed in several suggestive positions and Polaroids were taken before he placed it, for dismemberment, in the tub. Dahmer would often kiss and talk to the head as he took the remaining parts of the body apart. He wrapped part of the leg flesh, biceps, and heart in plastic and then froze them for consumption later. He then boiled the rest of the organs and flesh in Soilex until it became a jelly like substance, which helped him to rinse the flesh off, which he was planning on keeping. He then placed the bones, for 24 hours, in a light bleach solution and let them dry on clothes for a week to preserve them. He placed the severed head in the fridge before he removed the flesh and painted it with enamel.

On September 24, three weeks after Miller's murder, Dahmer met David Thomas, 22 and a father, at the Grand Avenue Mall. He was able to persuade him to come back to his apartment for some drinks, with promised money if he would pose for photos. After he was arrested, he would tell police that after he had given Thomas the sedatives, he didn't feel attracted to him, but he didn't want to awaken in case he became angry. Instead, he strangled and dismembered him, intentionally not keeping any of his body parts. He still photographed the Dismemberment and kept the photos, which help with the identification of Thomas.

After David Thomas' murder, Dahmer went five months without killing anybody, but he did try, at least five times, to lure men to his apartment between October 1990 and February 1991. He also often told his probation officer that he had feelings of depression and anxiety throughout 1990. He would often reference his financial problems, sexuality, and his solitary life. He also mentioned suicidal thoughts on a few occasions.

Dahmer noticed Curtis Straughter, 17, at a Marquette University bus stop in February 1991. Dahmer convinced him to come to his apartment by offering him money for nude pictures, with an added incentive of sex. Straughter was then drugged and then strangled with a leather strap. Once taken apart, Dahmer kept his genitals, skull, and hands and photographed every part of the process. Around two months later, on April 7, he met Errol Lindsey, 19, who was going to get a key cut. Lindsey was not a homosexual, but Dahmer was still able to convince him to go back to his apartment with him. Dahmer then drugged him and then drilled a hole into his head. Into this hole, he poured muriatic acid. Dahmer later said that Lindsey awoke and said "I have a headache. What time is it?" Dahmer had been trying to induce a permanent state of unresisting submissiveness. Dahmer then drugged Lindsey again and strangled him. After decapitating him, he kept the skull and skinned the flesh off of Lindsey's body. He placed the skin into a salt water solution for several weeks hoping that it would help to retain it. Reluctantly, he had to dispose of the skin when he noticed that the skin had became brittle and frayed.

The other residents of the apartment building started complaining about the smell coming from Dahmer's apartment, as well as the sound of a chainsaw and falling objects. Sopa Princewell contacted Dahmer about the complaints on different occasions. On one occasion Dahmer said the odors were because his freezer had quit working which caused everything inside to spoil. On a different occasion, he said that the odors were coming from the fact that some of his fish had just recently died.

Dahmer met Konerak Sinthasomphone, 14, on Wisconsin Avenue on May 26, 1991. He offered the youth money if he would go back to his apartment and pose for Polaroids. Sinthasomphone was the younger brother of the boy that Dahmer had molested back in 1988. He was initially reluctant, but he changed his mind and did go back to Dahmer's apartment. He had the boy posed for some pictures before he was drugged and Dahmer had oral sex with him. Jeffrey then drilled a hole into his head and placed muriatic acid through it into the frontal lobe.

Just before the youth became unconscious, Dahmer took him to his bedroom where Tony Hughes, 31, laid naked on the floor. Dahmer had killed him three days earlier. Dahmer said he "believed that Sinthasomphone saw his body," yet the boy didn't react to the bloated corpse. This was likely due to sleeping pills and the acid that Dahmer had put in his skull. After the boy became unconscious, Dahmer laid next to him drinking before he left to go to a bar and buy more alcohol.

When Dahmer was returning home, in the morning hours of May 27, he saw the boy at the corner State and 25th, naked and speaking in Laotian. There were three angry women standing close to him. Jeffrey walked up to them and lied to the women saying that Sinthasomphone, who he made up a name for, was his boyfriend, and tried to walk away from him. The women dissuaded him and told him that they had called 911. When officers Joseph Gabrish and John Balcerzak arrived, Dahmer's attitude relaxed. He told them that the boy was 19 and his boyfriend. He also said that he had been drinking and that they had a fight, and would often act this way if he's drunk. The women became annoyed and tried to show the officers that there was blood coming from Sinthasomphone's buttocks and that he had tried to get away from Dahmer when he tried to take him away, the officer harshly told the women they need to "butt out," and to "shut the hell up." They said the incident was domestic.

Even though the three women protested, the officers placed a towel around Sinthasomphone and took him back to the apartment, where Dahmer showed the police the semi-nude Polaroids he had taken earlier to verify their relationship. The officers later said that they noticed a strange smell, something like excrement, inside his apartment. The odor was caused by the decomposing body of Hughes. Dahmer later stated that all the officer did was peek around the door of the bedroom, but didn't investigate. The officers then left and told Dahmer to take care of Sinthasomphone.

If the officers had actually performed a background check on Dahmer, they would have found out that he was a child molester and currently on probation. After the officers had left, Dahmer injected more muriatic acid into the body, and on this occasion it proved fatal. The next day, Dahmer took the day off work so that he could devote the day to dismembering the bodies of Hughes and Sinthasomphone. He kept both of their skulls.

Dahmer traveled to Chicago on June 30 where he met Matt Turner at the bus station. Dahmer offered Turner a professional photo shoot if he would travel back to Milwaukee with him. Once back at his apartment, Dahmer drugged, strangled, and then cut his body. He put Turner's internal organs and head in plastic bags and placed them in the freezer. Nobody ever reported Turner missing. Five days after Turner's murder Dahmer brought Jeremiad Weinberger, 23, back to his apartment, and promised to spend the weekend together. After he had drugged Weinberger, he injected his head twice with boiling water, which eventually sent the man into a coma, from which he died two days after.

Jeffrey met Oliver Lacy, 24, on July 15 on the corner of Kilbourn and 27th. Oliver agreed to pose nude for Jeffrey and returned to the apartment and engaged in some tame sexual activities after which Dahmer drugged him. Dahmer tried, this time, to prolong Lacy's life instead of killing him right away. After he was unsuccessful when trying to render Lacy unconscious using chloroform, he asked for a day off from work, this was allowed, but he got suspended the next day. Dahmer strangled Lacy and then had sex with the body before he dismembered him. He placed the skeleton in the freezer and then the heart and head in the refrigerator.

On July 19, four days later, Dahmer found out that he had been fired. After he had received this news, Dahmer brought Joseph Bradehoft, 25, to his apartment. After strangling him, Dahmer placed a sheet over him and left him lying on the floor for around two days. When Dahmer took the sheet off on July 21 and found the head was covered in maggots. He then decapitated him, cleaned the head, and refrigerated it. He later acidified the torso with the torso of the two victims he had killed in the last month.

## Victims

In total, it is believed that Dahmer killed 17 men and boys between the years of 1978 and 1991. Of the 17 murders, 12 was committed in his apartment, three of them happened at his grandmother's, his second at the Ambassador Hotel, and his first at his home in Bath. The ethnicity of 14 of his victims had various minority background, and nine of them were African American. Dahmer claimed that the race of the victims meant nothing and that he went by their body and who he was attracted to.

Most of the victims were drugged and then strangled, although the first, Steven Hicks, was killed by strangulation and bludgeoning, the second victim was beaten to death, and then another victim, Ernest Miller, dying from blood loss and shock from his carotid being cut. Many of the 1991 victims also carried holes bored into their skull, through which Dahmer would inject boiling water or muriatic acid. At least three of these would prove fatal, but none of the occasion was this what Dahmer was trying to do.

### 1978

Steven Hicks, 18, on June 18. Dahmer found him hitchhiking to Chippewa Lake Park for a concert. Jeffrey admitted that what attracted him to Hicks was that he was shirtless. Dahmer beat and strangled him using a dumbbell before dismembering him. His bones were scattered behind the house.

### 1987

Steven Tuomi, 25, on November 20. He was murdered in a room at the Ambassador Hotel. Dahmer cannot remember this murder, but he did say he must have beaten him while drunk. Dahmer dismembered his body in his grandmother's house and placed the remains in the garbage. The police were never able to find his remains.

## 1988

James Doxtator, 14, on January 16. Dahmer met him outside of a bar. Dahmer lured him to his grandmother's house on the pretext of getting $50 if he posed for nude photos. Dahmer strangled him and kept him stored for a week in the basement before he was dismembered, and the remains were discarded in the garbage. Another victim where the remains were never found.

Richard Guerrero, 22, on March 24. He was strangled and drugged in Dahmer's bedroom at his grandmother's house. Dahmer dismembered him in the basement, disposing of the bones by dissolved them in acid in the basement. He cleaned and kept the skull for a while before getting rid of it. Remains were never found for this victim.

## 1989

Anthony Sears, 24, on March 25, 1989. Sears was the last person that Dahmer strangled in his grandmother's house, and was the first that Dahmer kept a body part. He kept the genitals and skull and was found in a filing cabinet in his apartment on his arrest.

## 1990

Raymond Smith, 32, on May 20. This was the first killing at Dahmer's apartment. Dahmer met Smith, a male prostitute, at a local tavern. After consuming a laced drink, he was strangled on the kitchen floor. Dahmer spray-painted, and kept his skull.

Edward Smith, 27, on June 14. This victim was a known to be acquainted with Dahmer, and he was last seen with him at a party. Dahmer ended up acidifying his skeleton. He unintentionally destroyed the skull when he placed it in the oven. They didn't find any of his remains

Ernest Miller, 22, on September 2. Dahmer met Miller, who was a dance student, just outside of a bookstore. Jeffrey said he like Miller's body. Dahmer cut his throat and took him apart in the tub. Dahmer kept his skeleton in a filing cabinet and froze parts of his legs, biceps, and heart for later consumption.

David Thomas, 22, on September 24. Dahmer met Thomas close to the Grand Avenue Mall. Dahmer lured him to his place with the promise of money. After Dahmer had drugged him, he decided he wasn't his type, but still strangled him and took pictures of the dismemberment process. Police were unable to find his remains.

## 1991

Curtis Straughter, 17, on February 18. They met at Marquette University bust stop. Once at his apartment, Dahmer strangled Straughter after drugging him. Then he was taken apart in the tub. Dahmer kept his genitals, skull, and hands.

Errol Lindsey, 19, on April 7. This was the first person that Dahmer tried his "drilling technique" on. This is where he would drill holes into their skull and would inject muriatic acid into the victim's brain. Dahmer said that Lindsey became conscious during this, after which Dahmer rendered him unconscious again, giving him another laced drink, and then strangled him. Lindsey was then skinned and Dahmer kept his skin for a while. Lindsey skull was recovered when Dahmer was arrested.

Toney Hughes, 31, on May 24. Dahmer lured Hughes, a deaf-mute, to his apartment with the promise of money for photos. They communicated with written notes. Dahmer strangled him and left his body to decay for three days. Dahmer dismembered him. Dahmer photographed the complete process. They found his skull and identified him by using his dental records

Konerak Sinthasomphone, 14, on May 27. Dahmer injected the youth with muriatic acid, and Dahmer left him alone to buy beer. Dahmer found him disoriented and naked on the street. Three women had called the police, but Dahmer was able to convince them that they were lovers and that the boy was only drunk. The police took him back to Dahmer's apartment. Dahmer again injected him with muriatic acid, which proved fatal. He kept his head and dismembered his body.

Matt Turner, 20, on June 30. Jeffrey went to the Chicago Pride Parade on June 30 and met Turner at the bus stop. He convinced him to return to Milwaukee to participate in a photo shoot. Dahmer then gave him a laced drink, strangled, and then took about the body in the tub. He placed his internal organs and head in the freezer. He then placed the torso in a 57-gallon drum of acid.

Jeremiah Weinberger, 23, on July 5. Dahmer met him at a Chicago gay bar, and he convinced him to return to his Milwaukee apartment to stay the weekend. This time, Dahmer injected his victim with boiling water. Dahmer would later say that his death was amazing because he died with his eyes still open. After cutting off his head, he kept the body for a week in the tub before he took him apart. The torso was stored in a large drum.

Oliver, Lacy, 24, July 15. Dahmer was able to lure the bodybuilding enthusiast to his apartment by promising him money for being his model. Dahmer drugged and then strangled Lacy using a leather strap. He was then decapitated, and the heart and head were placed in the fridge. Dahmer kept his entire skeleton to be a part of his shrine.

Joseph Bradehoft, 25, July 19. The last one of Dahmer's victims, Bradehoft was from Minnesota, and a father of three. He had been looking for work in the Milwaukee area when he was murdered. Dahmer left his body on his bed for two days. Then on July 21, Dahmer decapitated him. Dahmer stored his head in the refrigerator and then placed the torso of Bradehoft in the large drum.

## Modus Operandi

When talking about Dahmer's modus operandi, it's important to note that he often drank during the murders. He would start at home; continue at the bar, and then more when he brought the victim home. He also drank after the killing and during dismemberment. After years of drinking, he had developed a resistance to alcohol, and to make sure that he never lost control, he would drink only beer.

Before he set out to find a victim, Dahmer took the time to meditate and fantasize about the possible scenarios, how he would approach them, but most of all, he would think about the man that he wanted to meet and what all he would do to him. One of his favorite places to hunt was at shopping malls, along with the street, gay stores, or gay bars.

Typically he would go to places that were dedicated to gay men, but he didn't spend the entire hunting for his victim. He would enjoy the night, drink, and talk to other people, all while patiently waiting for his victim. This normally took place on Friday so that he would have the weekend to get rid of the body.

Once he found his possible victim, he would go up to them and ask them to come home whether to pose for photos, money for favors, have a drink, or have sex. He started out nice, charming, friendly, and seducing. He wanted to gain their trust so that all of the resistance and mistrust would disappear. The technique worked fairly well because he said that one out of three people that he would approach at the mall would accept his invitation and return home with him, and at the bars, the ratio was typically two to three.

He would often wear yellow contact lenses. He used these to remind him of his favorite movies and characters: the Emperor in "The Return of the Jedi" and "The Exorcist III," both of which had yellow eyes that gave them power. They were also noticed by other people.

After his proposal was accepted, they traveled back to Jeffrey's place, where he then would offer them a drink that was laced with sleeping pills. The victim would be unconscious within a half an hour. Sometimes, by this time, he would already be engaging in sexual activities. He would often lie next to the body after they were unconscious and listen to them breathe.

After they were unconscious, Dahmer would strangle his victims using his hands or a leather strap. The reason he always drugged the victim before killing them was that he didn't want to feel as if he was hurting them. Despite the fact he was killer, he didn't want to cause suffering. His main goal was only to have complete control over the body.

The victim's death did not matter to Dahmer; it was only a means to an end, so he tried his best often kill them quickly. He found no pleasure in the killing, and he often tried to find ways around killing them, but he was never successful. Thus he killed them as soon as he could.

Most of the time, after the victim died, he would have sex with them either through penetration, fellatio, and sometimes through a cut that he made above the pubic area. He would masturbate on the entrails after he began skinning the body. He was extremely fascinated by the entrails colors and would get turned on by the heat that came off the corpse.

Before cleaning, he would take pictures, so he was able to remember everything that had happened during the murder. Then he would dismember the body while taking photographs of the process. He would slice down from the sternum to the pubic area, and remove their internal organs. He would then slice off the meats starting with the calves and thighs. Then he would decapitate the corpse and place it in the fridge or freeze until he was ready to boil it. He would mix soilex in some water and use that to clean the skull. This process took about an hour.

He had tested a lot of different acids and chemicals so that he could make the body completely disappear. When he dissolved the different parts, all that would be left was a black and smelly residue that he would flush. Everything he did took place in his apartment, and by the time he was done, nothing would be left of the victim except for the parts he kept as souvenirs.

After the skulls were skinned, he would paint them gray so that they appeared to be made of plastic. He would also pose the victim's bodies for photos before he started the dismembering.

## Part 3: The Discovery

## Arrest

Dahmer approached three men on July 22, 1992, and offered them $100 to go back to his apartment and pose for photos, keep him company, and have a beer. One of the three Tracy Edwards, 23, agreed to go. When they entered Dahmer's apartment, Edwards noticed the foul odor and the boxes containing muriatic acid littered across the floor. Dahmer claimed that he used them for cleaning bricks. After some conversation, Dahmer had Edwards look around at his fish and Dahmer then placed handcuffs around his wrist. Edwards started to question what was going on, and this caused Dahmer not to be able to cuff him properly. Jeffrey then led Edwards to the bedroom for some pictures. Once in his bedroom, Edward noticed posters of nude men. Edwards also noticed that there was a large blue drum which a foul odor was coming from.

Dahmer then grabbed a knife and told Edwards he was going to take nude pictures of him. Wanting to calm Dahmer down, Edwards took off his shirt and told Dahmer he could take the pictures if he took the handcuffs off of him and sat the knife down. Dahmer then started watching TV. Edwards noticed that Dahmer began to rock back and forth and chanted something before turning away from him. Dahmer laid his head back onto Edwards's chest and started listening to his heart, then, held the knife against Edwards. He told Edwards that he planned on eating his heart.

While still trying to keep Dahmer from hurting him, Edwards continued to tell him that he was his friend and wasn't going to go anywhere. Edwards had already decided, given the opportunity, he would run at the front door or jump out the window. When Edwards told Dahmer he had to go to the restroom, he asked if it would be alright for them to sit in the living room and have a beer, where the air conditioning was. Dahmer allowed this, and they walked back to the living room once Edwards came out of the bathroom. Once back in the living room, Edwards watched Dahmer and waited until Dahmer had stopped paying attention before he asked him to go back to the restroom. When Edwards got up, he saw that Dahmer no longer had the knife. Edwards took this chance to punch Dahmer and knocked him off balance before heading out the door.

At 11:30 PM, Edwards flagged down two police officers. The officers saw that Edwards wore a handcuff around his wrist, to which Edwards told them some freak had tried to handcuff him and wanted them to remove the cuffs. The officers' key wouldn't fit the cuffs, and Edwards told them that he would take them back to where the guy had kept him for five hours.

Dahmer invited them all inside and said he did place the cuffs on Edwards, although he didn't explain why. Edwards then told the officers that Dahmer had threatened him with a large knife. Dahmer didn't comment and indicated to Rolf Mueller that he kept the key on a table next to the bed. Mueller went into the bedroom to retrieve the key, but Dahmer tried to pass him, which led for the other officer, Robert Rauth, to tell him to back off.

Mueller noticed that a large knife was lying underneath the bed, and saw a drawer open that housed several Polaroid pictures of bodies during the dismemberment process. He was able to discern that the photos were taken in the apartment. He took them to the officer and said, "These are for real." Once Dahmer noticed Mueller with the pictures, he fought the officers; trying to resist arrest. Officers were able to overpower him, cuffed him, and then called a second squad car. Mueller opened the fridge and found a freshly severed head sitting on the bottom. While pinned on the floor Dahmer looked up at the officers and said, "For what I did I should be dead."

After a further investigation by the Criminal Investigation Bureau, they found four severed heads in the kitchen. They found seven skulls, some of which were bleached and some painted, in the closet and bedroom. In the fridge, they found two human hearts, a tray that collected blood drippings, part of an arm muscle. In the freezer, they found organs, flesh, and torso that were frozen to the bottom.

In another area, they located severed hands, two skeletons, two preserved penises, and scalp. Inside the blue drum, they found three torsos in acid. There were 74 photos that detailed the dismemberment of all of the men. The chief medical examiner said, regarding the recovery of the victims, that "It was more like dismantling someone's museum than an actual crime scene."

During the early morning hours of July 23, 1991, Detective Patrick Kennedy interviewed Dahmer about the murders and the evidence they found in his apartment. For a little over two weeks, Detective Murphy and Kennedy interviewed Dahmer for a combined 60 hours. Dahmer didn't have a lawyer present during this time. He explained that he wanted to confess; and said, "I created this horror and it only makes sense I do everything to put an end to it." He admitted that he had killed 16 men in since 1987 in Wisconsin, along with Steven Hicks' death in 1978 in Ohio.

He explained that most of his victims had been unconscious before their death, but some had died because of boiling water or acid being injected into their brain. Since he couldn't remember Tuomi, he didn't know if he was unconscious, but he did say it was possible that after he saw him naked, while drunk, he tried to rip out his heart.

Most of the murders after he moved into his apartment had a ritual aspect to them. He admitted that he performed necrophilia with many of the bodies; and performed sexual acts with their viscera while he was dismembering the body. Dahmer would take out the organs, then suspend the body to drain out the blood, before dicing up the organs he didn't want to keep and removing the flesh from the body. He would either acidify or pulverize the bones he didn't want to keep. He also confessed to eating parts of the thighs, biceps, livers, and hearts of several of the victims.

When asked about his increase in the rate of killings over the past two months, he said that he had been "completely swept along." He also added that "It was an incessant and had a never-ending desire to be with someone at whatever cost. Someone good looking and really nice looking. It just filled my thoughts all day long." Then the detectives questioned him about seven skulls and two complete skeletons, Dahmer explained that he had been working on constructing an altar of victims' skulls. He had planned on placing this on the black table in the living room where he had photographed his victim's bodies. The skulls would be adorned on either side with Oliver Lacy and Ernest Miller's skeletons on each side. He was going to remove the flesh from the four heads in the kitchen, and they too would be used on the altar, as well as the skull of a future victim.

He would place incense both ends of the table, and he was going to set a blue lamp up. He was going to place the construction in front of a window covered with an opaque black shower curtain, and Dahmer would sit in front of it in a black leather chair. On November 18, 1991, Dahmer was asked who he would dedicate the altar to, and he answered, "Myself... It was a place where I could feel at home." He said that the altar as an area where he could meditate, and he felt he could draw power. He added, "If this had happened six months later, that's what they would have found."

## Trial

Dahmer ended up being charged on July 25, 1991, with four murder charges. They then charged him with 11 more murders by August 22, that he had committed in Wisconsin. Investigators in Ohio, on September 14, had uncovered hundreds of fragments of bone in the woods behind the house he had lived in as a child, and Dahmer had confessed to killing his first. They were able to formally identify Steven Mark Hicks with a vertebra and two molars with X-ray records. Three days after the identification, Dahmer was charged with his murder.

Dahmer did not get charged with attempted murder of Tracy Edwards. He also didn't get charged with Steven Tuomi's murder. The main reason why he wasn't charged with Tuomi's death was that they wanted to be able to prove the murder beyond a reasonable doubt, and Dahmer didn't have any recollection of committing the murder, and there was no physical evidence that it ever happened. On January 13, 1992, at a preliminary hearing, Dahmer pleaded guilty on the grounds of insanity to 15 murder charges.

The trial began on January 30, 1992, and was overseen by Judge Laurence Gram. Since he pled guilty on January 13, he waived any right to trial and proven guilty. The main debate between the counsels was whether Dahmer suffered from a personality or mental disorder. The prosecution claimed that even if he did suffer from a disorder, it did not prevent Dahmer from enjoying his criminal acts; neither did it prevent him from him being able to resist his impulses.

The defense said that he was insane because of his necrophilic drive. An expert for the defense, Dr. Fred Berlin, believed Dahmer was unable to conform during the crimes because he suffered from necrophilia. Another expert for the defense, Dr. Judith Becker Professor of Psychiatry and Psychology, also diagnosed Dahmer with necrophilia. The last expert, Dr. Carl Wahlstrom a forensic psychiatrist, diagnosed him with a psychotic disorder, alcohol dependence, necrophilia, schizotypal personality disorder, and borderline personality disorder.

The prosecution argued that he was not insane. One expert, Dr. Phillip Resnick, believed Dahmer didn't have necrophilia because he wanted living partners as seen by the fact that he tried to create submissive and unresistant sexual partners. Another expert, Dr. Fred Fosdel, said that he believed that Dahmer didn't suffer from mental defect or disease while committing the murders. He went on to describe Dahmer as a cunning and calculating individual, able to know the difference between right and wrong, and he was able to control his actions. He did state that he thought Dahmer suffered from paraphilia, but he concluded that he wasn't a sadist.

The last expert, Park Dietz a forensic psychiatrist, testified that he believed that Dahmer did not suffer from mental diseases when he committed his crimes. He said there was also plenty of evidence that proved that Dahmer prepared in advance, meaning they weren't impulsive. He also believed the fact that Dahmer had to be intoxicated to kill was important. He stated that; "If he had a compulsion to kill, he would not have to drink alcohol. He had to drink alcohol to overcome his inhibition, to do the crime which he would rather not do." Dietz would diagnose Jeffrey with schizotypal personality disorder, paraphilia, and a substance use disorder.

George Palermo, a forensic psychiatrist, and Samuel Friedman, clinical psychologist, testified independently. Palermo believed that he committed the murders because of pent-up aggression. He called Dahmer a sadist and suffered from antisocial personality disorder, but was still completely sane. Friedman believed that Dahmer's killing was caused by a need for companionship. He believed Dahmer wasn't a psychotic and spoke kindly of him saying he was, "Amiable, pleasant to be with, courteous, with a sense of humor, conventionally handsome, and charming in manner. He was, and still is, a bright young man." He said he had a personality disorder that was not otherwise specified and featured sadistic and obsessive-compulsive traits.

After two weeks, the counsels gave closing arguments on February 14. Each counsel could speak for two hours. The defense went first and kept drawing from the testimony of the mental health professionals. Boyle said he was sick and lonely person and couldn't conform to societal ways

The prosecution then delivered their closing remarks where McCann described him as sane, and in complete control of his actions, who only strove to be undetected. His murders were an act of hatred, frustration, resentment, anger, and hostility, and that his victims "died merely to afford Dahmer a period of sexual pleasure." McCann finished by stating that he believed Dahmer was trying to escape responsibility by pleading guilty on the grounds of insanity.

Court reconvened on February 15 for the verdict. They found Dahmer to be sane and that he didn't suffer from any disorders, but in every count two of the jurors would signify dissent. His first two counts sentenced him life imprisonment plus ten years, and the rest carried a mandatory 70 years in prison. Wisconsin had abolished the death penalty in 1853, so that wasn't an option for this case.

After his father, Lionel, and stepmother Shari had heard about Dahmer's sentencing, they requested a ten-minute private meeting before he was sent to Columbia Correctional Institution in Portage. Their request was granted, and they exchanged well-wishes and hugs before he was taken away.

Three months later he was extradited back to Ohio to stand trial for Steven Hicks' murder. The hearing lasted for 45 minutes, and Dahmer pled guilty and sentenced to 16th life imprisonment.

## Part 4: After

## Prison

For his first year in prison, he stayed in solitary confinement because they were worried about Dahmer's safety. With the consent of Dahmer, after a year, he was taken to a less secure cell. He then was given the work detail of cleaning the toilet block.

After he had confessed to the murders, he asked the detective for a Bible. He was given a Bible, and he decided to become a devoted Christian. He also started reading creationist books after his father's urging. Roy Ratcliff baptized Dahmer in May 1994.

Ratcliff continued to see Dahmer every week after he was baptized, until later in 1994. Dahmer talked to him about death, and ask if he was sinning just because he was living.

Another inmate, Osvaldo Durruthy, tried to kill Dahmer by cutting his throat with a shank made from a toothbrush. Dahmer was returning to his cell after his weekly church service with Roy Ratcliff, when this happened. He only received superficial wounds and received no serious injuries. Dahmer's family said that he had been ready to die for a long time, and was willing to accept any punishment that he may go through while in prison. He had regular contact with his father, stepmother, and his mother, Joyce. He hadn't even seen his mother since 1983 at Christmas. Joyce later told the media that when she called him each week, she would ask about his well-being, Dahmer would say something like, "It doesn't matter, Mom. I don't care if something happens to me."

## Death

On November 28, 1994, Dahmer headed for his work detail. Along with him was Christopher Scarver and Jesse Anderson. The three of them were left without supervision for around 20 minutes. Guards found Dahmer around 8:10 AM on the floor of the gym bathroom with facial and head wounds. A 20-inch metal bar was used to beat him along the face and head. At some point during the attack, Dahmer had struck the wall. At the time, Dahmer was still living. They quickly got him to the hospital where he died an hour later. They also found Anderson beaten in the same manner Dahmer had, and he died two days later from injuries he suffered. Scarver had already been serving a life sentence because of a 1990 murder. He informed the police that he first attacked Dahmer while he was cleaning up the staff locker room, and then he went after Anderson as he was cleaning locker room for the inmates.

Scarver claimed that Dahmer didn't make a sound or fight while he was attacked. Immediately after the attack, Scarver went back to his cell and said, "God told me to do it. Jesse Anderson and Jeffrey Dahmer are dead." He kept telling the authorities that he never planned the attack, but he did tell investigators that he concealed a 20-inch bar, which he used to carry out the murders.

Joyce, Dahmer's mother, responded angrily after learning about her son's death. The incident gained mixed reactions from the families of the victims but most of them appeared to be happy with his death. The prosecuting attorney in the Dahmer case warned the public about making Scarver out of the hearing, saying that he still murdered two people. Scarver was sentenced to two more life sentences on May 15, 1995. Even though Scarver had confessed that he had concealed the weapon in 1994, he changed his statement in 2015 and said that the murders were caused by a confrontation where one of the men had poked him. In this new information, Scarver said that the two laughed at him when he turned around because of the poking before they left to clean separate rooms. Scarver then followed Dahmer into the locker room.

Scarver said that before he murdered Dahmer, he asked him about a newspaper article detailing his crimes, and asked whether they were true. He continued to say that Dahmer's crimes revolted him and that he didn't think Dahmer seemed sorry about the murders. He continued by saying that Dahmer would taunt the inmates and employees by making his food look like body parts and would even add ketchup for blood. Even though the prison knew that Scarver hated Dahmer, they deliberately left them unsupervised so that he would be able to kill him. Furthermore, Scarver said that Dahmer had to have a guard escort him around whenever he left his cell because he was so disliked that he would be attacked anytime.

In Dahmer's will, he asked that there would be no service and to be cremated. They cremated Dahmer's body in September 1995, and the ashes were split between his parents.

## Aftermath

11 of Dahmer's victims' families sued for damages and were awarded part of Dahmer's estate. In 1996, the lawyer that represented eight of the victim's families, Thomas Jacobson, said that they planned to auction off Dahmer's. The relatives said that the motivation for this wasn't greed motivated, but it still caused controversy. Milwaukee Civic Pride, a civic group, was brought together to try and raise funds to purchase and destroy anything that remained of Dahmer's possessions. This civic group brought together $407,225, and Joseph Zilber donated $100,000 for purchasing the estate. Five of the families that Jacobson represented came to an agreement over the terms, so they destroyed the possessions and the sent them to an undisclosed landfill.

A candlelight vigil was held on August 5, 1991. This was intended to heal and celebrate the community and over 400 people attended. Present were family members of many of the victims, gay rights activists, and community leaders. They said that the vigil was to enable the people of Milwaukee to "share their feelings of pain and anger over what happened."

The apartment building where 12 of the victims were killed, at 924 North 25th Street, was demolished in November 1992. Only a vacant lot stands there. Different plans to turn the area into new housing, a playground, or a memorial garden have failed to come to fruition.

Jeffrey Dahmer's name came back into the spotlight in August 2012, almost two decades since his death, when it was announced that his childhood home in Bath, where he murdered Steven Hicks, was on the market. The current owner, Chris Butler a musician, said that it would make a wonderful home for somebody, as long as they could get past what had happened.

Christopher Scarver, the inmate who murdered Dahmer and Anderson, received two additional life sentences. He continues to serve time in the Centennial Correctional Facility in Colorado. In 2005, Scarver tried to bring a civil suit against the guards and staff of the Wisconsin Secure Program Facility. He said that he had been subjected to cruel punishment. He said he had to spend 16 months in solitary confinement as a result of murdering Dahmer. A judge dismissed the case stating that he found that the actions of the other officials were not unlawful in any way. Scarver appealed the decision, but the decision was upheld in 2006. Barbara Crabb, a federal judge, ordered that Scarver, along with around three dozen other mentally ill inmates be moved to a facility in Wisconsin. Scarver was eventually moved to Centennial Correctional Facility.

As agent speaking for Scarver announced in 2012 that he was willing to write a book detailing the killing of Dahmer.

Lionel retired as an analytical chemist and continued to live with his new wife Shari, in Ohio. Lionel has always been a big advocate for creationism, and Shari is part of the Medina County Ohio Horseman's Council board. Neither of them wants, or feels they should, change their last name, and have never lost their love for Jeffrey even after everything he did. *A Father's Story,* a book written by Lionel, was published in 1994, and he donated part of his earnings to the victims' families. The majority of the families showed Shari and Lionel their support, but three ended up suing Lionel. Two of them sued him because he used their names without obtaining consent. The other, the family of Steven Hicks, sued Joyce, Lionel, and Shari, in a wrongful death suit, citing parental negligence was the cause of death.

In November 2000, Joyce Flint died of cancer. Before her death, she tried to commit suicide at least one more time. David, the younger brother of Jeffrey, has changed his last name and continues to live happily in anonymity.

## Conclusion

Thank you for making it through to the end of *Serial Killers*. I hope you enjoyed all the information found within these pages.

Finally, if you found this book useful in any way, a review on Amazon is always appreciated!

# Serial Killers

*The True Story of Serial Killer Jeffrey Dahmer, "The Milwaukee Cannibal"*

# Table of Contents